This book belongs to:

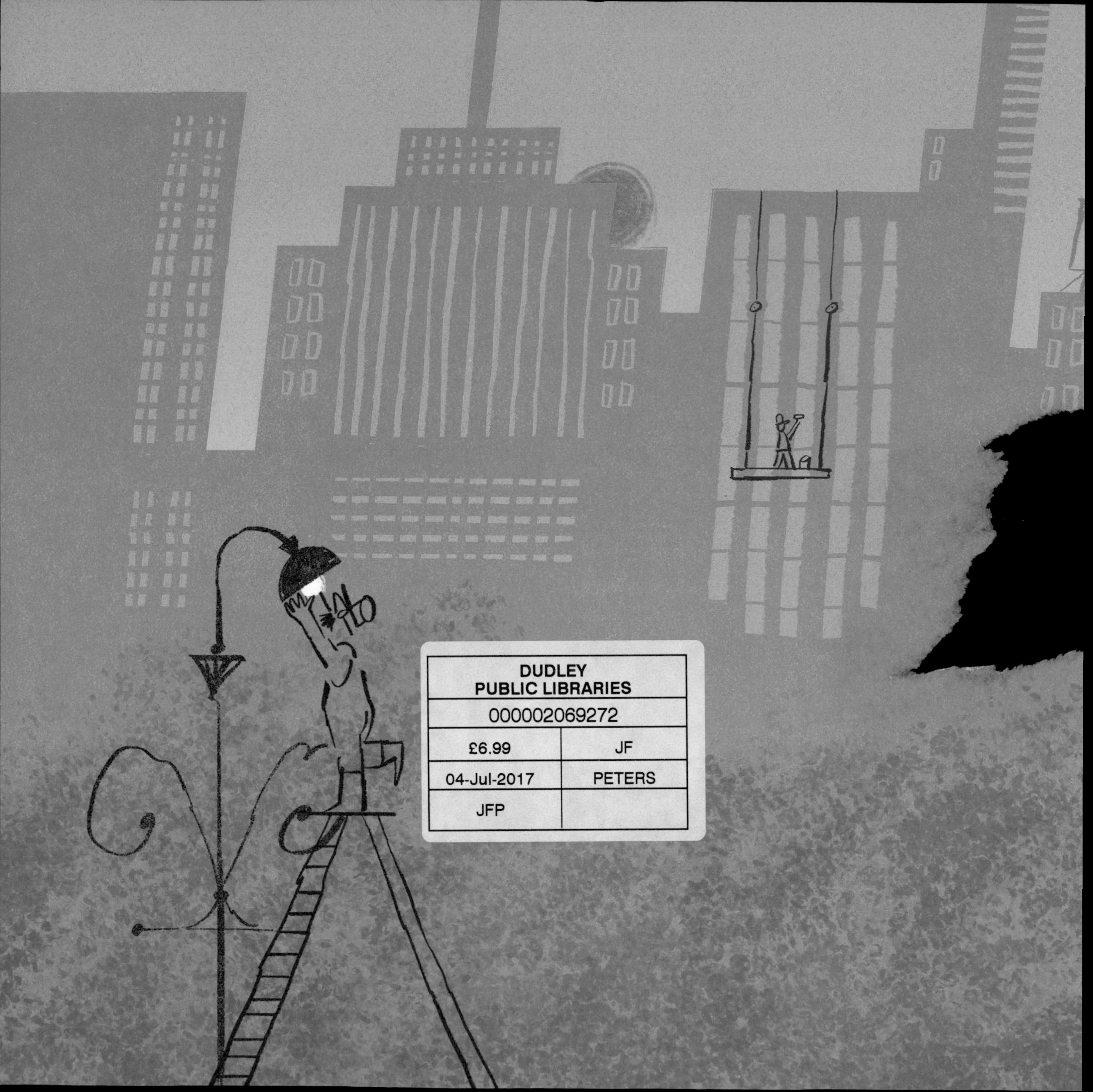

A note for grown-ups

Oxford Owl is a FREE and easy-to-use website packed with support and advice about everything to do with reading.

Informative videos

Hints, tips and fun activities

Top tips from top writers for reading with your child

Help with choosing picture books

For this expert advice and much, much more about how children learn to read and how to keep them reading ...

OXFORD
UNIVERSITY PRESS

Great Clarendon Street, Oxford OX2 6DP
Oxford University Press is a department of the University of Oxford. It furthers the University's objective of excellence in research, scholarship, and education by publishing worldwide. Oxford is a registered trade mark of Oxford University Press in the UK and in certain other countries

First published 2017

British Library Cataloguing in Publication Data: Data available

ISBN: 978-0-19-274798-3

1 3 5 7 9 10 8 6 4 2

Printed in China

Paper used in the production of this book is a natural, recyclable product made from wood grown in sustainable forests. The manufacturing process conforms to the environmental regulations of the country of origin.

FOR MARK, AMY AND MEL xxx – J.C.
FOR MY MUM. AS THE SONG SAYS,
YOU ARE THE BEST OF ME. – L.

. . . where Fetch, Madison, and Zachary were waiting, because that's what they wanted more than anything, too.

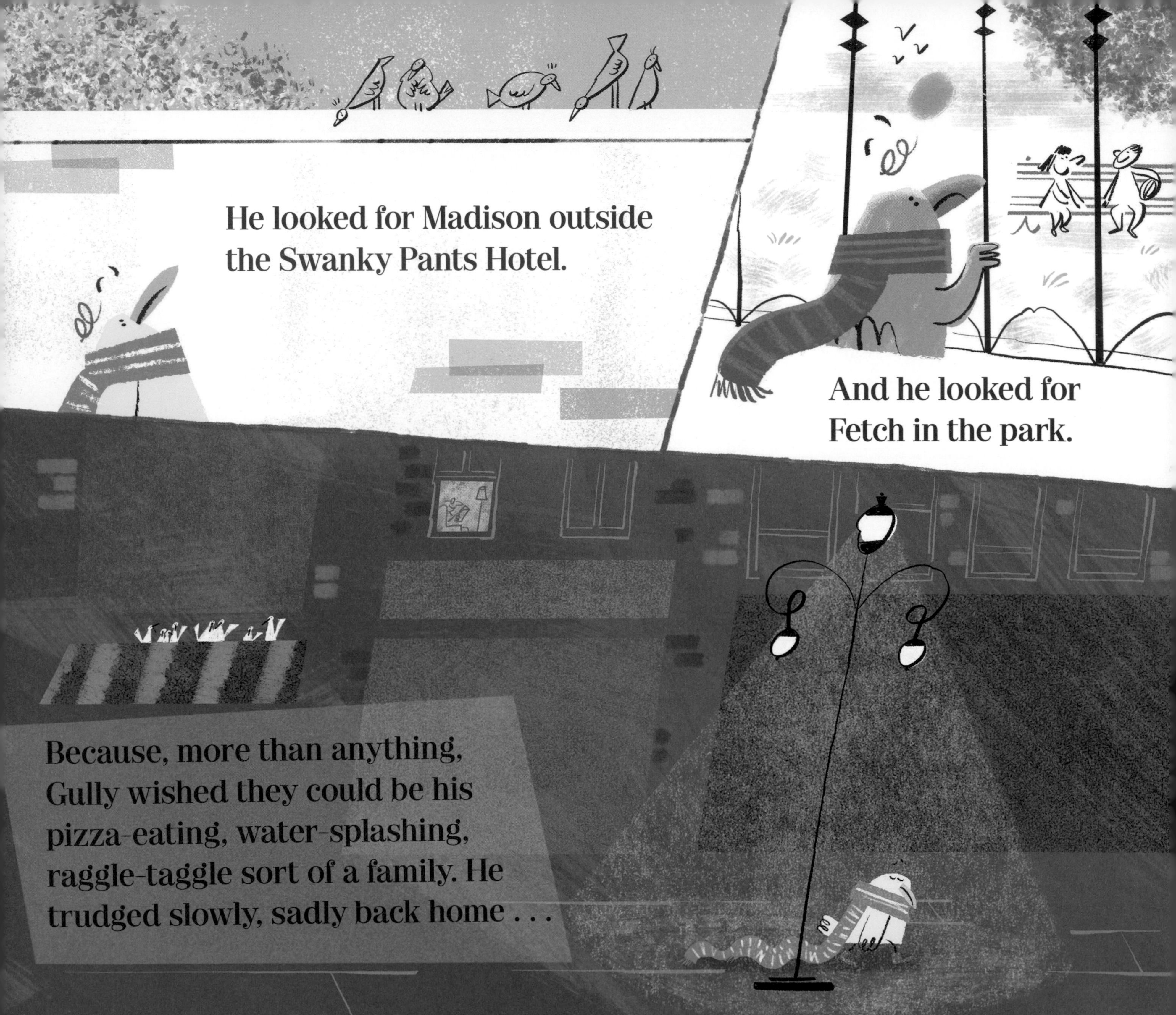

He looked for Madison outside the Swanky Pants Hotel.

And he looked for Fetch in the park.

Because, more than anything, Gully wished they could be his pizza-eating, water-splashing, raggle-taggle sort of a family. He trudged slowly, sadly back home . . .

The next day Gully woke up in his new home. His feet felt warm. His feathers felt dry.

'Balloon!'

But he didn't have everything he needed.

He looked for Zachary in the library.

Then Zachary, Madison, and Fetch slipped quietly into the night.

Zachary found a door and opened it for Gully.
'I think this could be just the home you're looking for,'
he said. 'And it won't get swept away.'

After cheesy-saucy-sticky pizza
it was time to get washed . . .

and dried.

'Mmm. Cheese and tomato, family-sized. Tuck in!' said Zachary. 'Family . . .' whispered Gully.

'I think,' said Zachary,
that everything you need
is right here.'
'How wonderful!' said Gully.

Zachary led the way. 'A home for Gully,'
he said thoughtfully. 'Follow me.'

In a quiet corner they met a
clever-but-not-at-all-dull sort of a rat.
'I'm Zachary,' said the rat.
'Can I help you find a book?'

'Actually, I'm looking for a home,' said Gully.
'A warm, dry one that won't be swept away.'

'Let's go inside for a rest,' said Madison.

And walked
some more.
CITY
LIBRARY

Gully and Fetch followed Madison round the city.

They walked and walked.

'You didn't stay long,' said a haughty, don't-touch-me-but-underneath-I'm-nice sort of a cat who'd been watching from a wall.

'No,' said Fetch. 'There was no home for Gully in there.'

'I'm Madison,' said the cat, 'and I know every street in this city. Come on, I'll help you.'

But seagulls and sausage dogs weren't welcome.

It could have made a wonderful home.

On the other side of the street, Gully and Fetch found a grand hotel that looked warm and dry.

HOTEL
Paaaaaarp!
'This traffic is terrible!'
Honk!
Paaaaaarp!
Parp!
'Get outta the way!'

But it wasn't safer outside.

And noisy. And busy.

‘A home that doesn’t get swept away, where my feet are warm, my feathers are dry, and my tummy is full,’ said Gully dreamily.

'A tidy park is a happy park!'

They decided to look for Gully’s perfect home outside the park.

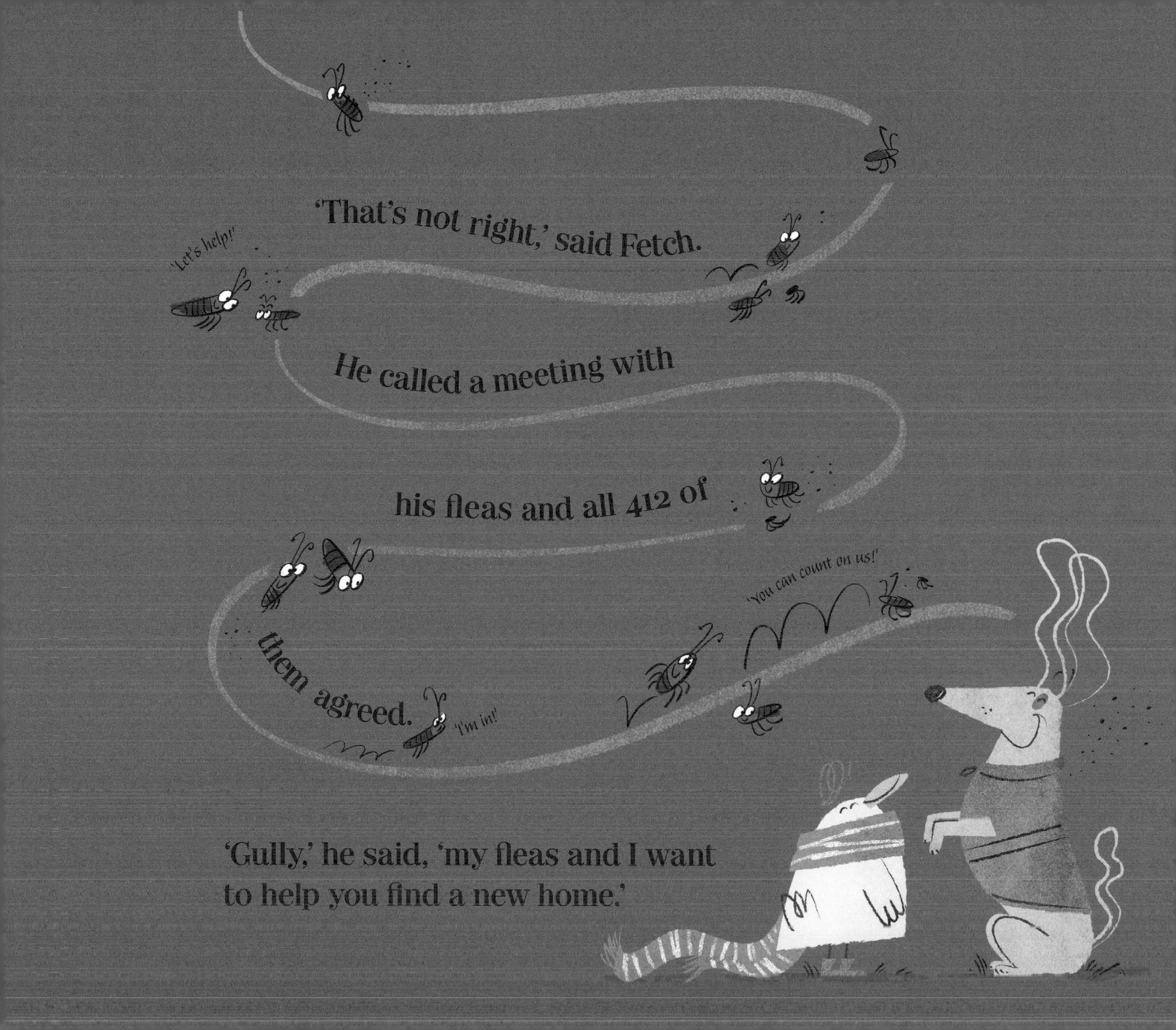

'That's not right,' said Fetch.

He called a meeting with his fleas and all 412 of them agreed.

'Gully,' he said, 'my fleas and I want to help you find a new home.'

'Your home is swept away *every morning*?'
said Fetch. 'That's terrible!'

Gully giggled at the surprised look on
Fetch's face. 'Every morning. But I always
build a new one by bedtime.'

. . . lolloped up to Gully.

'I'm Fetch,' he said. 'I fetched your stick.'
'Oh, thank you,' said Gully. 'I'm Gully.
But I didn't throw the stick.
You see . . . my home was swept away.
It happens every morning.'

'Hello birdy!'

'Oh, what a beautiful morning!'

Then, one morning, a messy, raggle-taggle, friend-to-fleas sort of a dog . . .

**Every day, at ridiculously early o'clock,
Gully's home was swept away.**

A Home for Gully
WRITTEN BY
JO CLEGG
ILLUSTRATED BY
LALALIMOLA
!
OXFORD
UNIVERSITY PRESS